ROYAL COUNTY OF BERKSHIRE LIBRARY AND INFORMATION SERVICE	CHURCHEND PRIMARY SCHOOL TILEHURST READING	
10 FEB 1992		

CLASS NO. J621.38 white

TO AVOID FINES THIS BOOK SHOULD BE RETURNED ON OR BEFORE THE LAST DATE STAMPED ABOVE. IF NOT REQUIRED BY ANOTHER READER IT MAY BE RENEWED BY PERSONAL CALL, TELEPHONE OR POST, QUOTING THE DETAILS DISPLAYED.

0749 602 724 2 097 03

TELEVISION AND VIDEO

© Aladdin Books Ltd 1990

Designed and produced by
Aladdin Books Ltd
28 Percy Street
London W1P 9FF

*First published in
Great Britain in 1990 by*
Gloucester Press
96 Leonard Street
London EC2A 4RH

ISBN 0-7496-0272-4

Design David West
Children's Book Design

Editorial Lionheart Books

Researcher Cecilia Weston-Baker

Illustrator Alex Pang and Ian Moores

Printed in Belgium

CONTENTS

The Working Parts	5
Different Types	6
The TV Set	8
The TV and Video Camera	11
Picture Signals	12
Video Tape and Recorders	15
Transmitting Signals	16
In the Studio	18
Outside Broadcasts	20
Special Effects	22
Video Discs	24
Special Systems	26
History of TV and Video	28
Glossary	30
Index	32

HOW · IT · WORKS
TELEVISION AND VIDEO
IAN GRAHAM

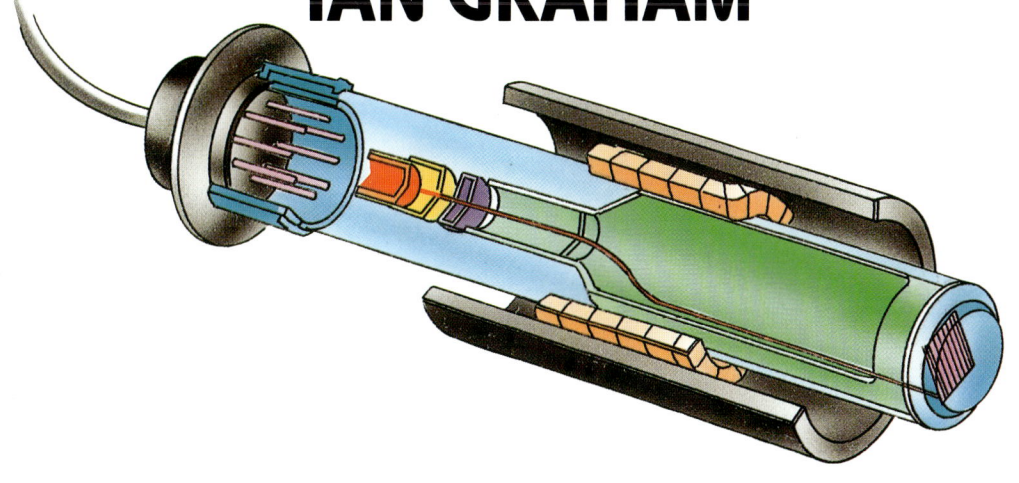

GLOUCESTER PRESS
London · New York · Toronto · Sydney

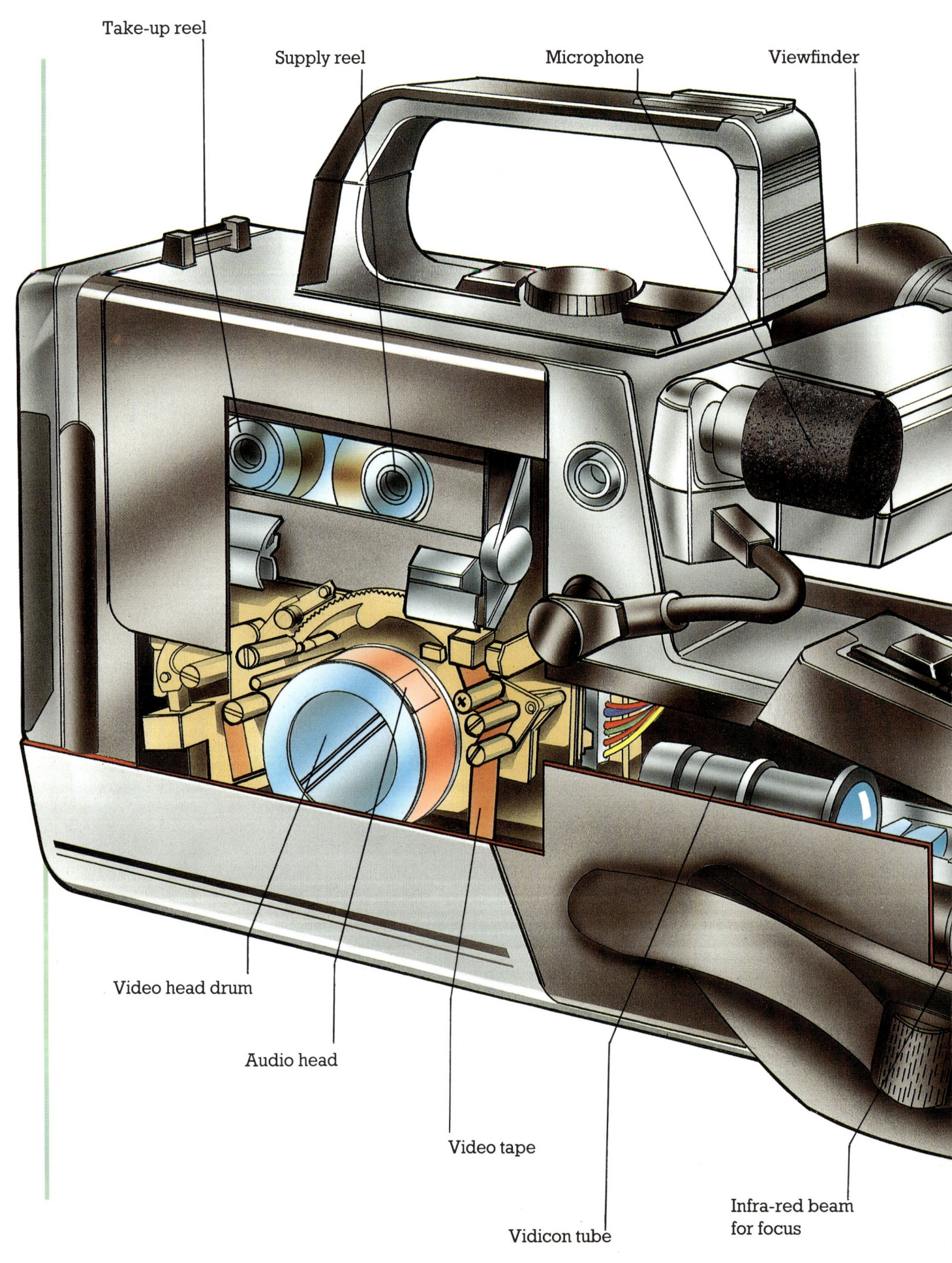

THE WORKING PARTS

A camcorder is a portable video camera and a video tape recorder combined in a single piece of equipment. It is designed to record full-colour moving pictures and sound on magnetic tape.

The image entering the lens is seen by looking through the viewfinder. This is actually a television tube, or monitor, with a tiny 3 to 4cm wide screen. Power zoom controls on the camcorder's hand-grip operate a motorized system for changing the lens's angle of view. In effect, this changes the lens focal length enabling both telephoto and wide-angle pictures to be recorded from the same position. Many camcorders also have an automatic focusing system. Infra-red beams sent out from and detected by devices on the front of the camcorder measure how far away objects are and control a motor that focuses the lens to produce a sharp picture.

The lens in the camcorder shown here focuses the image on to a "pick-up" tube. The tube converts the image into an electrical signal. The latest camcorders use a small sturdy device called a Charge Coupled Device, or CCD for short, instead of the larger fragile glass pick-up tube. Both devices do the same job. An image enters at one end and an electrical copy of the image comes out of the other end.

Once the image has been converted to an electrical form, it can be fed to the recorder part of the camcorder. At the same time, sound picked up by a microphone is also sent to the recorder. There, the two signals are stored on magnetic tape in the same way that, for example, pop music is recorded on cassette tapes. The recording can be played back at any time using the camcorder or another video recorder. To see and hear the recording, the camcorder or recorder is connected to an ordinary television set.

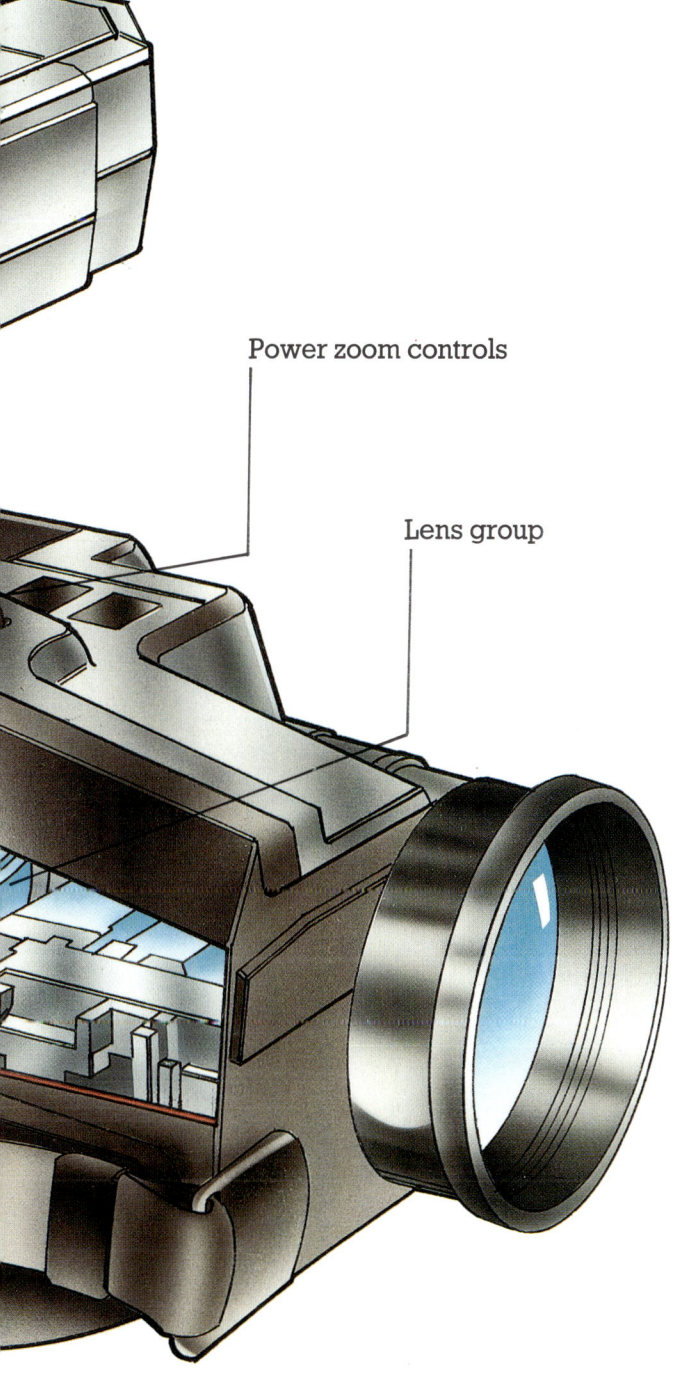

Power zoom controls

Lens group

DIFFERENT TYPES

There are many different types of television and video cameras and also video recorders and television sets. The equipment used by television companies is generally capable of better picture and sound quality than the equipment available to the majority of television viewers and home video users. However, the gap in standards of the results of professional programme makers and amateurs is gradually narrowing as the quality of home video equipment continues to improve.

Millions of homes all over the world now have a video recorder. Domestic video recorders are used in two ways.

The home video recorder has changed television viewing habits. People no longer have to watch programmes as and when they are broadcast. It is also possible to watch one television channel while recording another. Home video recorders can even switch themselves off using a built-in timer to record a programme when no-one is at home to operate the machine. A simple screen (above) is all that is needed, besides the recorder, to enjoy the video playback. While most home video recorders are bulky, amateur video cameras (above left) and portable televison sets (left) are getting smaller and smaller.

They enable television viewers to record programmes and watch them at a later time or date. Most movies made for the cinema are also available to buy or rent on video tape cassettes, and these can be played back in home recorders. Some TV and video equipment is made as small and lightweight as possible so that it can be carried about easily. To be truly portable, it must also be able to operate for long periods by battery power. Portable video recorders and camcorders are fitted with special battery packs that can be charged up again when they are exhausted.

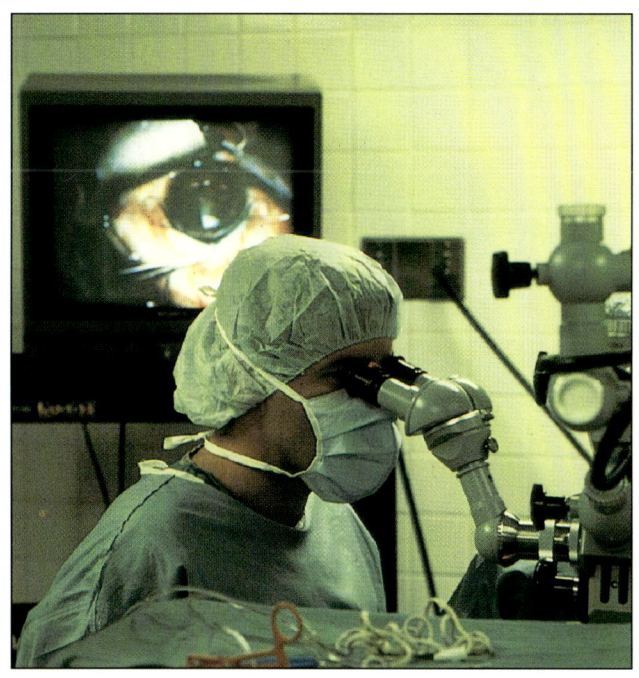

Video recordings play an important role in education. The technique of a skilled eye surgeon (above), for example, can now be viewed by many more students than could attend the operation. Similarly, students can study with video programmes. Cameras range in size and complexity from lightweight camcorders to the sophisticated varieties used by television companies for their studio or outside (above right) broadcasts. The Heli-tele (right) is a television system designed for use on aircraft. The spherical television housing is steered from inside the aircraft by a control joystick.

THE TV SET

A television, or TV set, is a device for converting television signals back into the pictures that originated the signals. It relies on the fact that any colour can be produced by mixing three basic, or primary, colours – red, green and blue – in different quantities. Three electron beams produced by electron "guns" continuously sweep across and down the inside of the screen. This is coated with stripes of materials known as phosphors, which glow red, green or blue when struck by electrons.

A perforated sheet of metal called a shadow mask ensures that each electron beam lands on a slightly different area of the screen. One beam strikes only red phosphors, one strikes only blue and the third strikes only green. The coloured dots are so tiny and so close together that our eyes see them merged together into a complete full-colour picture.

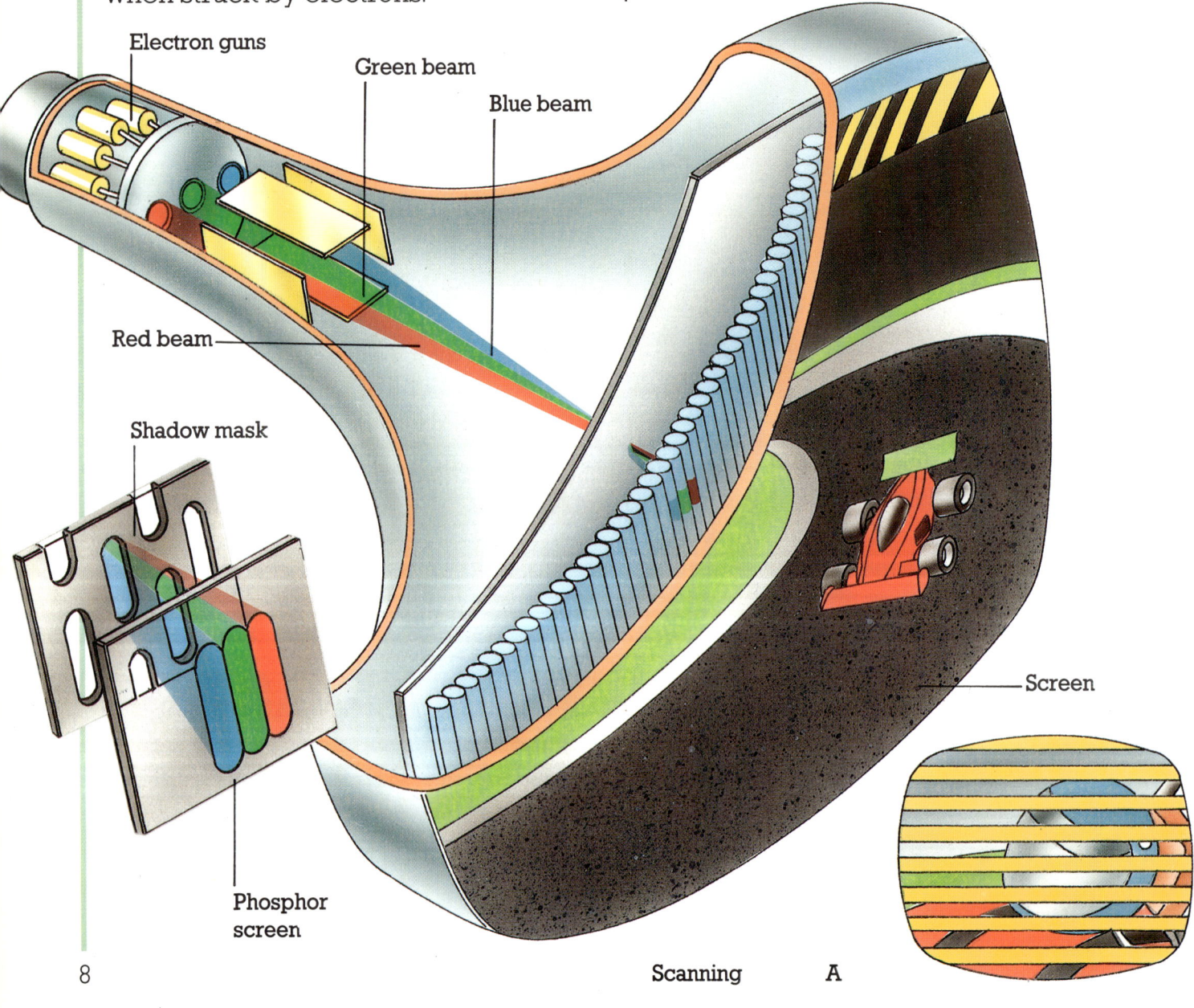

Scanning

The complex interior of a TV set, with the tube to the right in this photo.

Electrical signals consist of streams of tiny particles known as electrons. When the TV is switched on, the electron guns each produce a narrow beam of electrons. As the three electron beams scan the screen through the shadow mask, the phosphors they fall on glow (right) and give the impression of a lifelike image. The beams do not start at the top of the screen and trace out one complete picture at a time. First, the odd-numbered lines are scanned (A). Then the spaces between these lines are scanned (B) to fill them up (C). All this happens many times a second.

Video cameras are smaller now than ever thanks to the use of miniature pick-up tubes.

Light from an image entering a TV camera lens is focused through a glass block on to three pick-up tubes at the same time. One tube is sensitive to red light, one to blue and the third to green light. Inside the tube, an electron beam is swept across the target by a variable magnetic field provided by electromagnets round the tube.

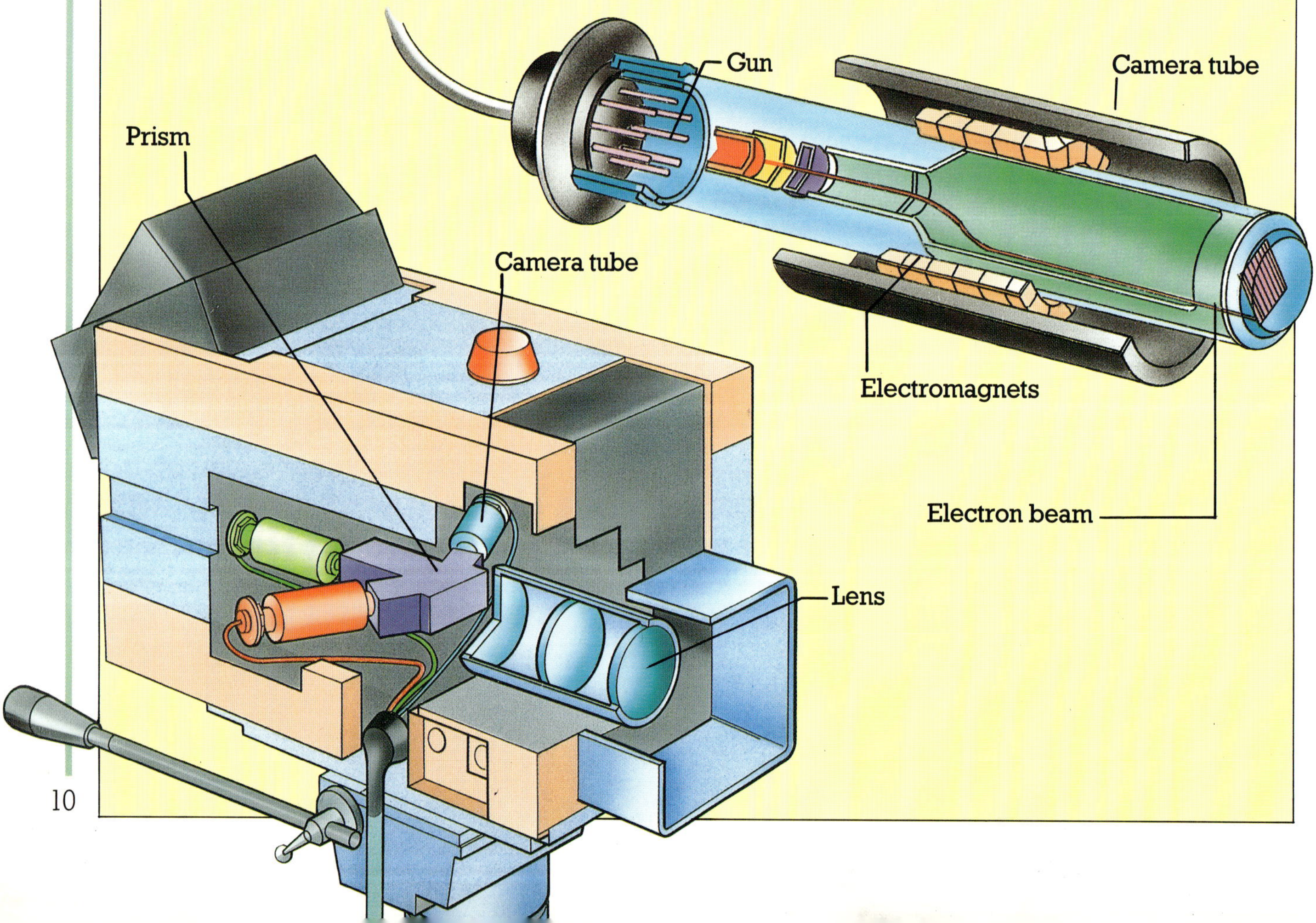

THE TV AND VIDEO CAMERA

The process of bringing television pictures into your home begins with the television camera. It converts the scene in a television studio, or at an event such as a football match, from a mass of light rays into a stream of electrical signals.

Television cameras rely on the ability of some materials to react to light by releasing electrons. These are vital for the operation of the camera's most important component, the pick-up tube.

Colour television cameras have three pick-up tubes, one for each of the primary colours – red, blue and green. One end of the tube, called the faceplate, is coated with the light-sensitive material. This is referred to as the target. Different types of tube use different target materials. One common type is a compound containing the elements selenium, arsenic and tellurium. Once the image has been transformed into an electrical signal, it can be processed and stored by other equipment.

The light-sensitive target at the front of a pick-up tube is charged up to a low voltage of around 30 volts (1). An electron beam scans the target (2). Light enables the charge to leak away (3). The brighter the light is, the more charge leaks away. An image focused on the target is transformed into a pattern of electric charges. As the electron beam scans the target, it soon restores each point to its fully charged state. The size of the charging current depends on how much light has fallen on the target at that point. A brightly lit point requires a much higher charging current (4) than a dimly lit point (5). The video signal is formed from this charging current.

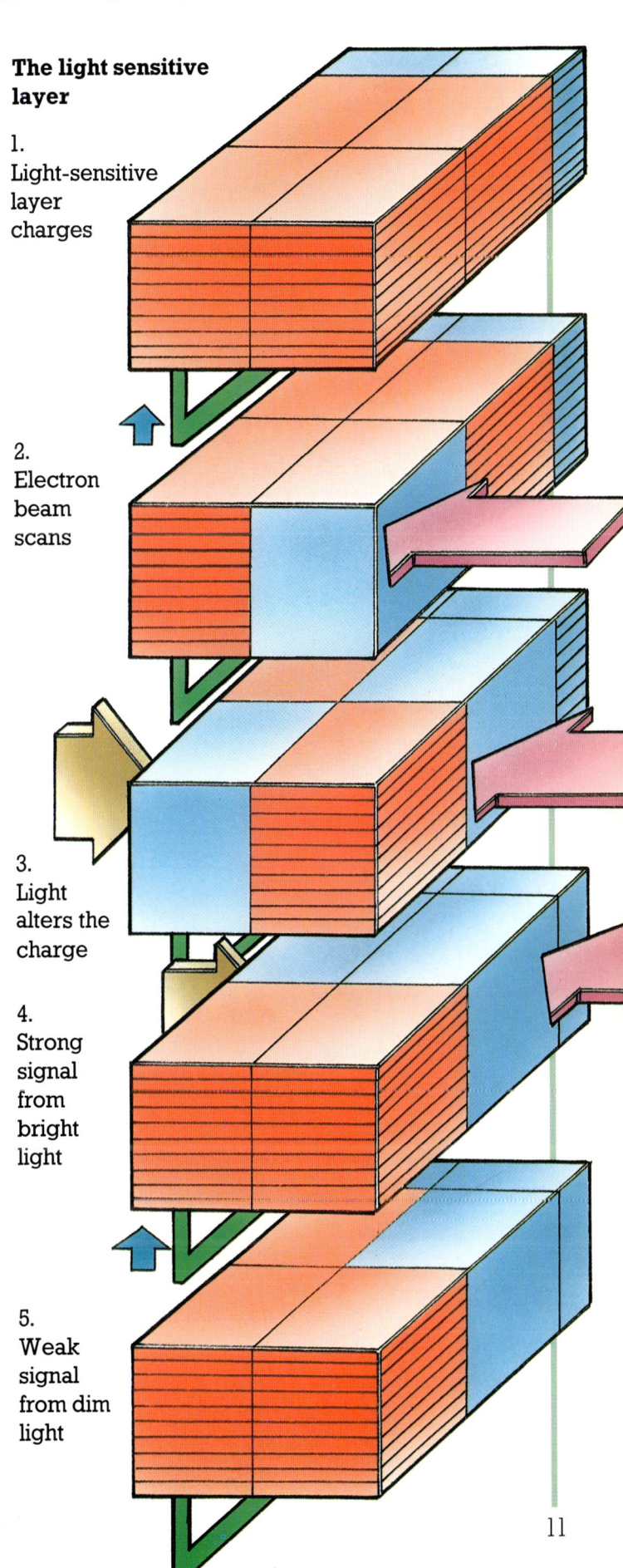

The light sensitive layer

1. Light-sensitive layer charges
2. Electron beam scans
3. Light alters the charge
4. Strong signal from bright light
5. Weak signal from dim light

PICTURE SIGNALS

Television picture signals may be obtained from any one of several sources. They may be received from a transmitter or relay satellite using an aerial, or directly from a broadcasting studio via an underground cable. They may come from a video tape playing in a home video recorder or a camcorder. They could originate from a video games player or a home computer.

Wherever the signals come from, they must be processed so that they can be fed into the television tube, the main image-forming component. TV sets are designed to receive television pictures in the form of a high-frequency radio signal. This incorporates a carrier wave used to transport the picture signals through space. It is added to the picture at transmission and removed by the TV set. Video recorders and games machines have a device called a modulator whose job is to add the picture signals to a carrier wave, a process known as modulation. Many TV sets now have direct video connections for video recorders, eliminating the unnecessary modulation process.

For many years the television set was a self-contained device for receiving broadcast television programmes picked up by a roof-top aerial (above far right). Nowadays, the TV set is becoming a display unit for pictures received from a wide range of sources including the video recorder (far right) or graphics unit (right), and also the computerized images created by TV games. Some games allow players to interact with the changing images on the screen (above right).

Recording on tape

A video head, the device responsible for recording pictures on video tape, is a tiny electromagnet made from an iron core with a coil of wire wound around it. When a video signal flows through the coil, it creates a magnetic field in the head. A narrow gap in the head interrupts the field. If magnetic tape is positioned close to the gap, the field can complete its magnetic circuit by flowing through the tape. Magnetic particles in the tape are magnetized by the field. A recorder's video drum normally uses two video heads. Each revolution of a head produces one field (half-section) of the picture. So each spin of the drum produces a complete frame. Stopping the tape results in a still picture.

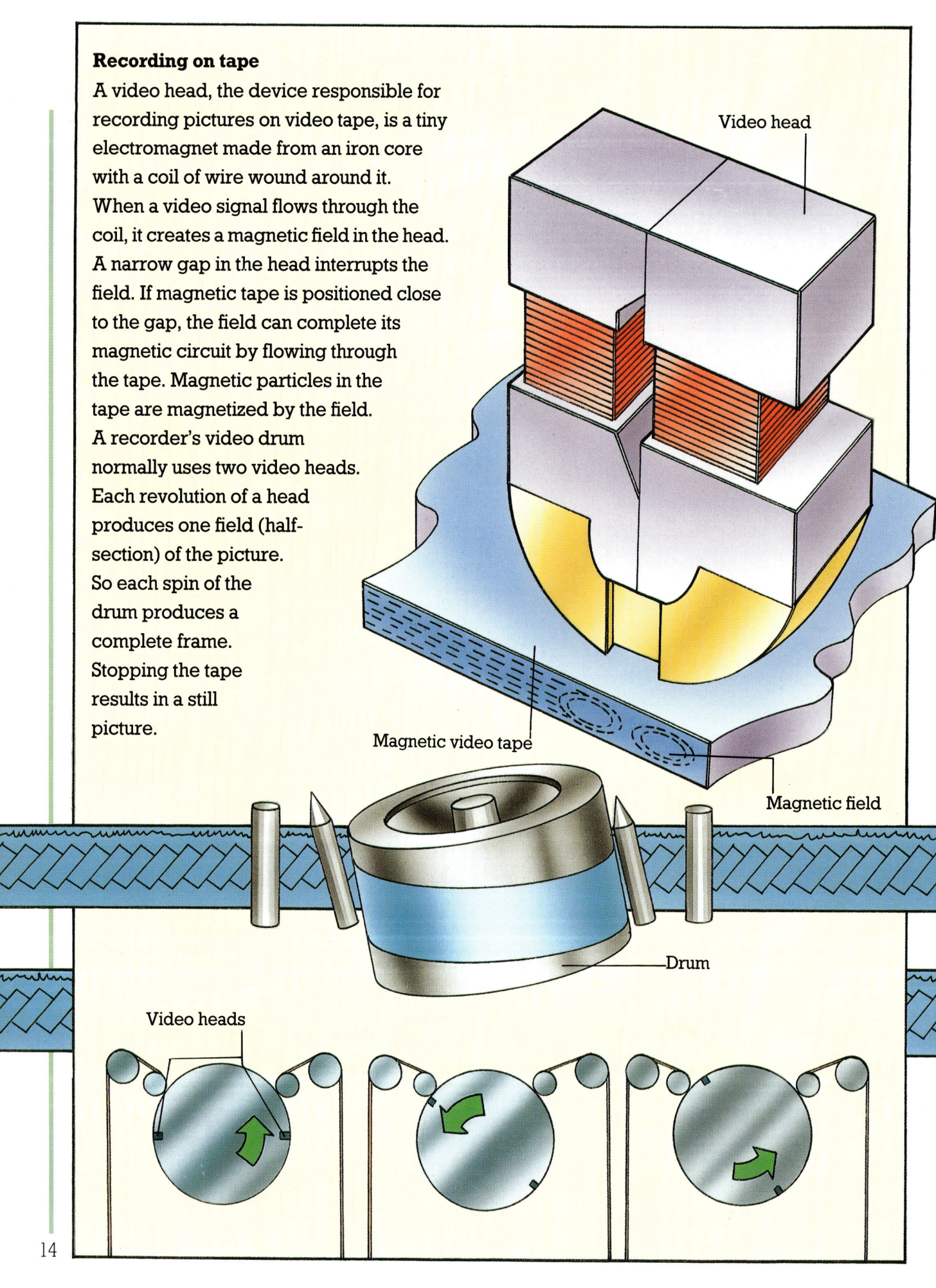

VIDEO TAPE AND RECORDERS

Recording television pictures on magnetic tape requires a high tape-speed because a vast amount of information must be stored quickly. The tape would have to travel at 5 metres a second, (5 m/s) – over 100 times faster than the speed of audio tape. This is impractical. The tape speed is kept down to just over 2 cm/s by a special scanning technique. The video heads that transfer the picture signals on to the tape are mounted in a spinning drum. In VHS, the most popular home video system or format, the drum spins at 1,500 revolutions per second in the opposite direction to the direction of tape travel. The drum is set at an angle and the tape is wrapped around more than half of the drum. The path of the video heads along the tape traces out a spiral shape, and this helps to provide the required video "writing" speed of almost 5 m/s.

A video editor at work.

Video recordings are rarely made to the same length of time or in precisely the same order as they are required to appear in the final programme. The process of shortening and rearranging sections into the desired time-span and order is called editing. Unlike film, which is edited by cutting it up and sticking it together again in a different order, video recordings are edited electronically. Chosen sections of the programme material are recorded in the correct order from the original tape on to a new tape.

Television programmes are distributed around the country by a network of main transmitters. The signals from these are picked up by relay stations which pass on and spread the signals locally on a different frequency. Growing numbers of viewers receive their programmes by satellite or from cable television stations. Satellite and cable offer additional channels to those put out (broadcast) by many TV studios.

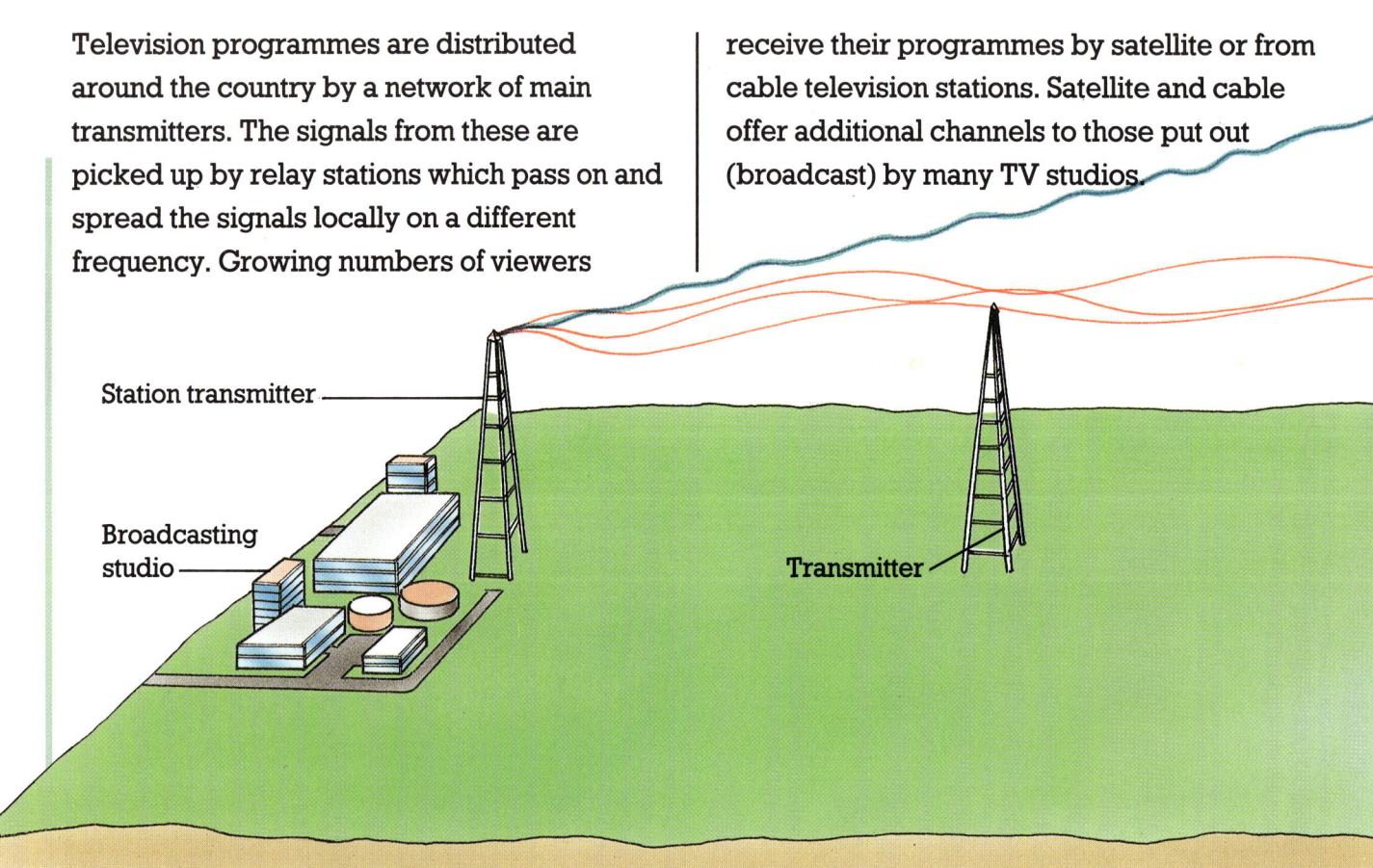

TRANSMITTING SIGNALS

When electrons vibrate, some of their energy forms electrical and magnetic effects, an electromagnetic field. If they vibrate quickly enough, the field can become separated from the circuit the electrons are flowing through and travel through space. This principle is used to transmit television signals. The low frequency picture signals are combined with a high-frequency radio wave called a carrier wave. This provides the necessary conditions for the signals to spread outwards from the transmitter.

Television signals flow around us invisibly all the time. They are received by pointing an aerial at the transmitter. The electromagnetic waves produce tiny voltages as they flow around the aerial. These are boosted in strength (amplified) and, in the television tube, converted back into the pictures and sounds that produced them.

Most television aerials resemble metal trees with a central trunk and branches. All the branches are usually lined up in the same direction to match the direction of signal being transmitted. There are now small dish-shaped aerials too. These are designed to concentrate the television signals relayed by a satellite in space on to a small pick-up suspended above the dish. Cable transmission does not require an aerial. A central cable TV station collects all the signals from ground transmitters, satellites and other sources and feeds them into homes along metal or fibre optic cables buried underground.

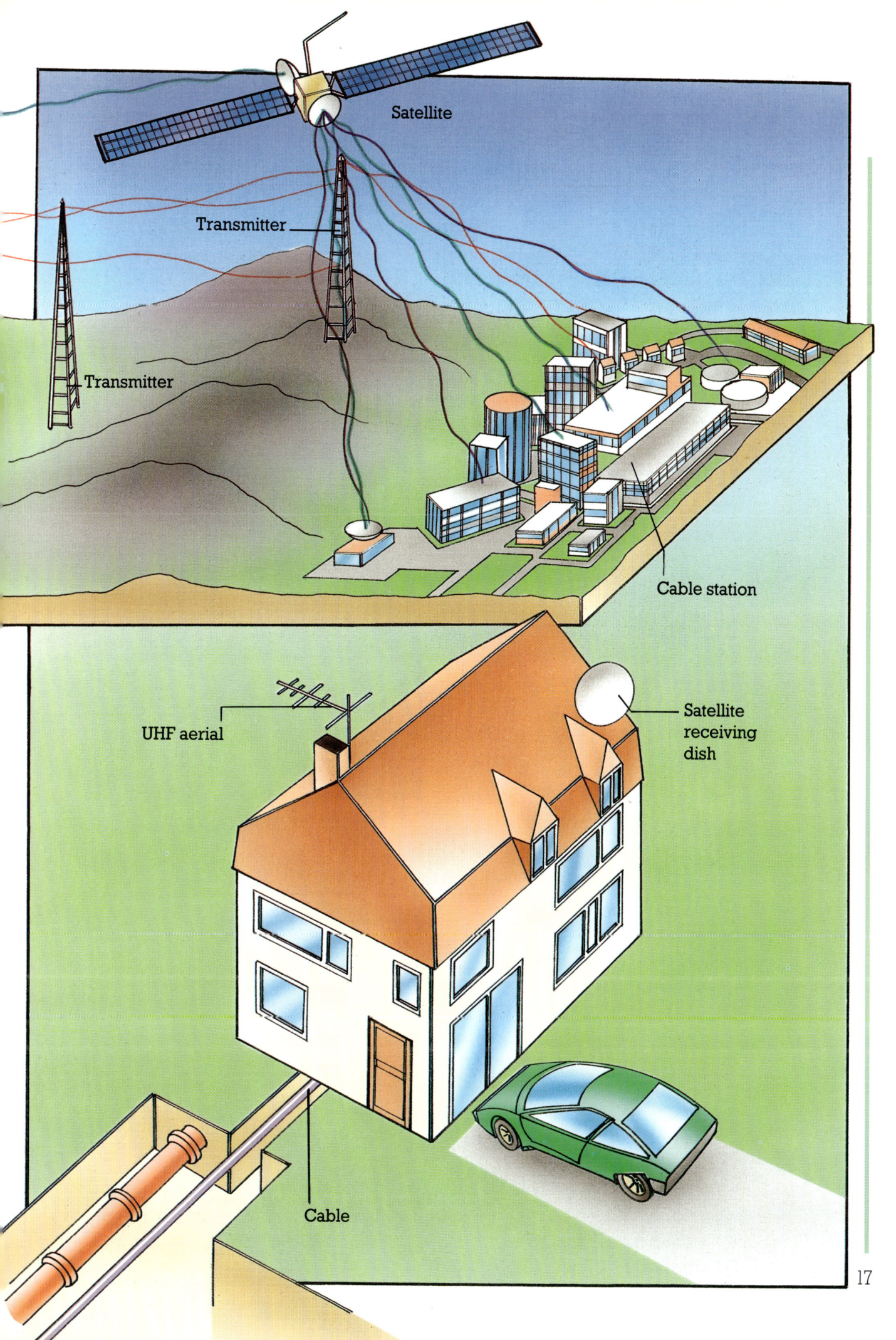

IN THE STUDIO

A television studio is a specially built complex where teams of people with a variety of broadcasting skills come together to produce TV programmes. Some of the television crew are skilled in designing sets, the settings created to surround the actors or programme presenters. Others operate machinery including cameras, lights and sound equipment. Another team of people direct all the cameras and control everything that happens in the studio during a recording.

When a programme has been made, the editors select the shots that will form the final recording. In drama productions, music and sound effects may be added to the programme too. Live transmissions such as news and chat shows are broadcast as they happen. This requires constant control and quick responses from everyone involved as there is no opportunity to stop and re-record anything that has gone wrong.

A television presenter is able to look directly into a camera while speaking long passages of text because the text is projected on to a glass screen on the front of the camera. This cannot be seen by viewers. The system is called teleprompt. Newsflashes – stories just received from reporters which have to be broadcast immediately – are read from typewritten notes in the normal way. Most presenters wear an earpiece for receiving messages from the director in the control room. A sports or news presenter may have to change the order of items in a programme while it is actually being transmitted by following instructions heard in the earpiece.

A news broadcast "on the air".

The programme's control room.

Teleprompt system used by T.V. presenters.

Four areas of activity are involved in recording a television programme such as a crime story. First, the *studio floor*, where the sets that the viewers will see are constructed and lights and cameras are set up. The programme's director, and other staff, including the vision mixer who ensures that images from different cameras are woven together in a suitable manner, control activities on the studio floor from the *control room*. In the *video control room*, engineers monitor the quality of the camera images. The sound is monitored and mixed by engineers in the *sound control room*.

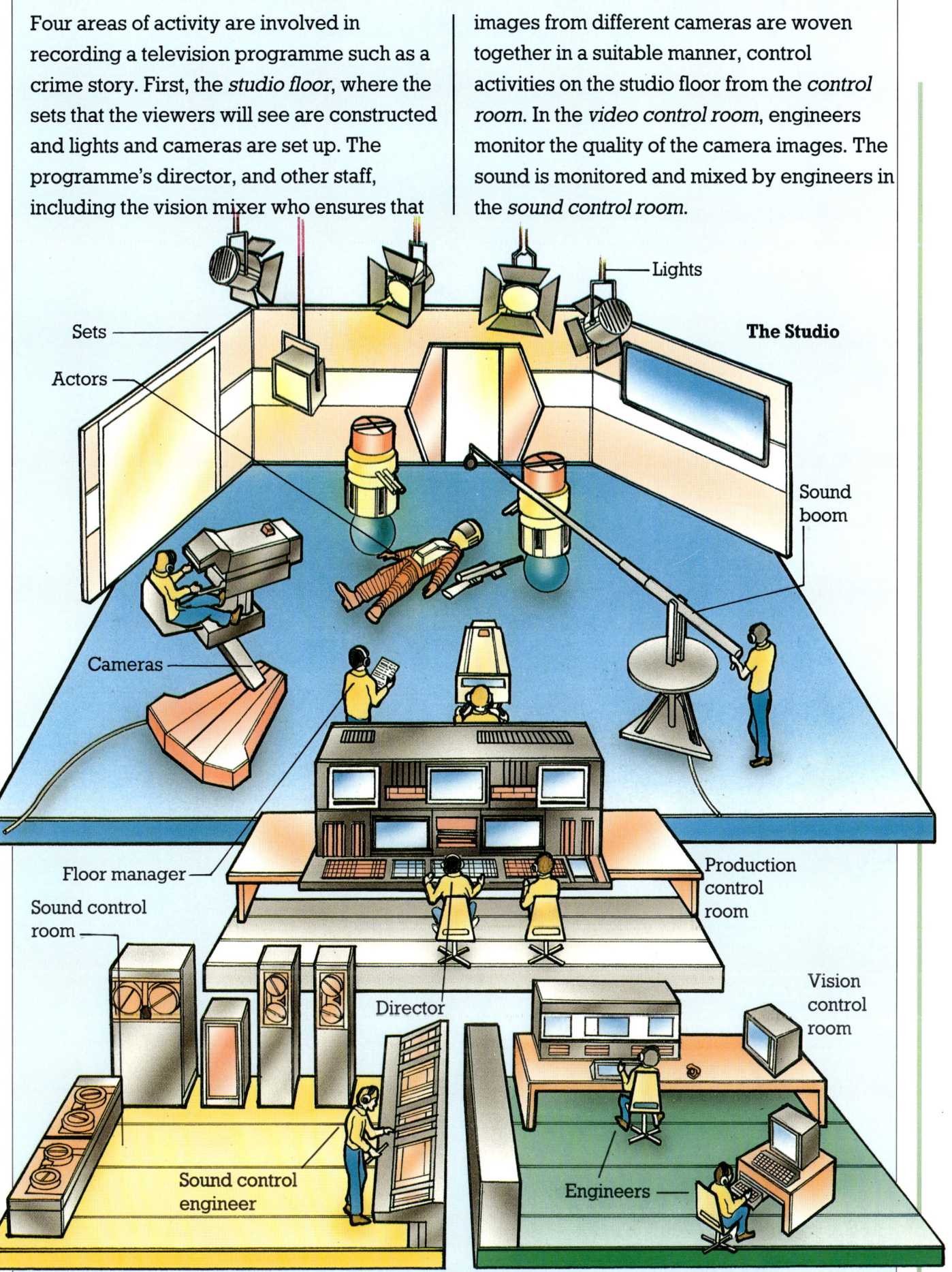

OUTSIDE BROADCASTS

Some programmes cannot be made in the controlled environment of a television studio. To record sports events, for example, the programme-makers must go to where the event is happening and set up an outdoor studio there. This is called an outside broadcast or OB for short.

A specially designed truck houses a mobile control room. Electrical power for its equipment is supplied by a generator. Cameras are set up at each important point around the event. Helicopters and airships are often used to fly cameras over an event. Pictures and sound from these camera positions are brought together in the control room. There, they may be recorded for future editing and transmission or they may be relayed to the broadcast studio for immediate transmission.

Signals can be sent to the studio in two ways. If the control truck is in line of sight contact with the studio or a relay station, the signals can be transmitted by short-wavelength radio waves called microwaves. News teams working in remote areas without a control truck can return recordings to the studio by satellite using a mobile transmitter.

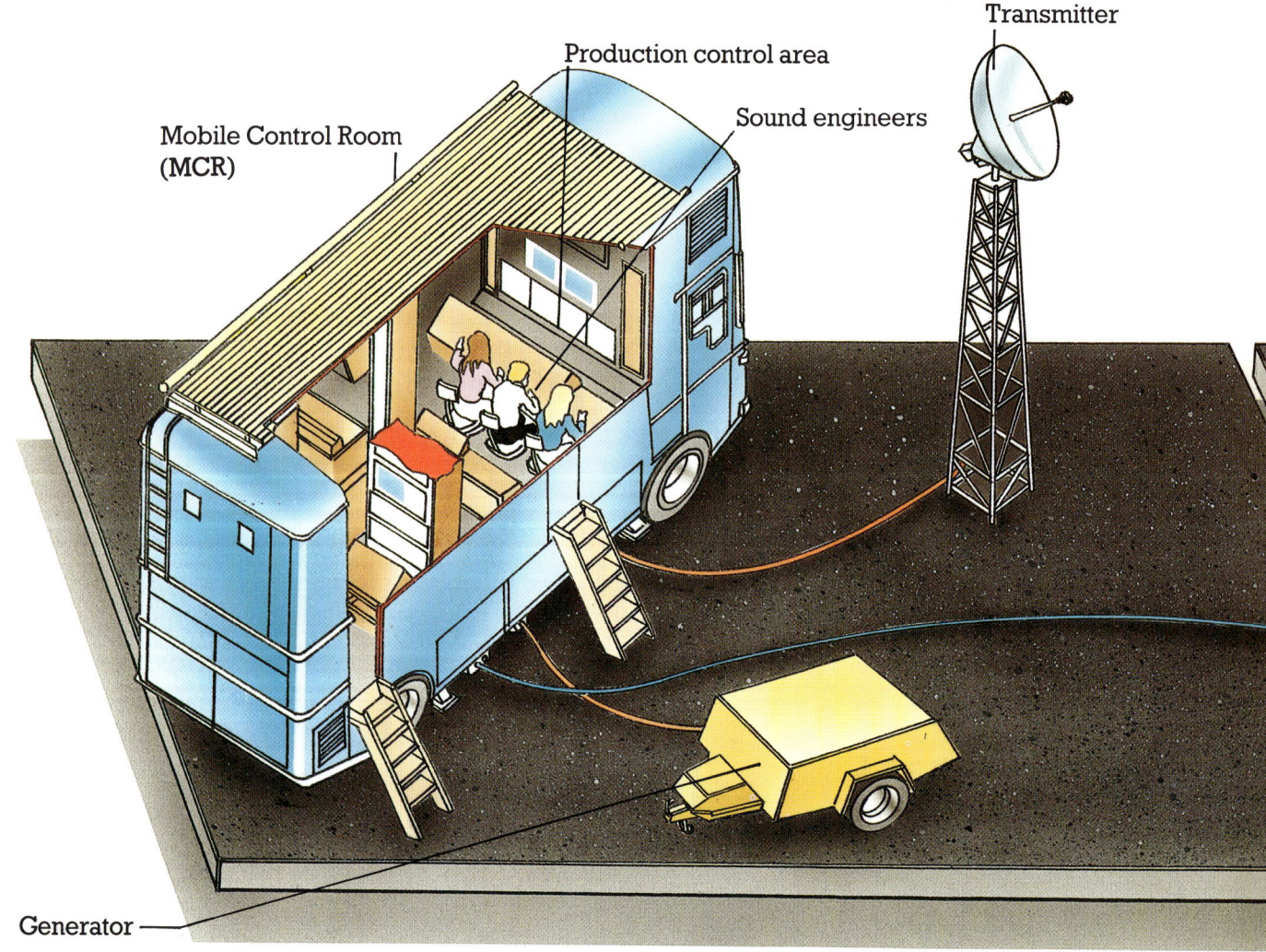

An Electronic News-Gathering (ENG) team make an interview on a street in China.

Pictures and sounds of an event are usually fed to the mobile control room by cable. Camera operators working in places where cables are difficult to use may carry their own compact transmitters, as do those on outdoor news teams (ENG cameramen). The signal from the control room may be sent back to the studio by microwave or relayed by communications satellite.

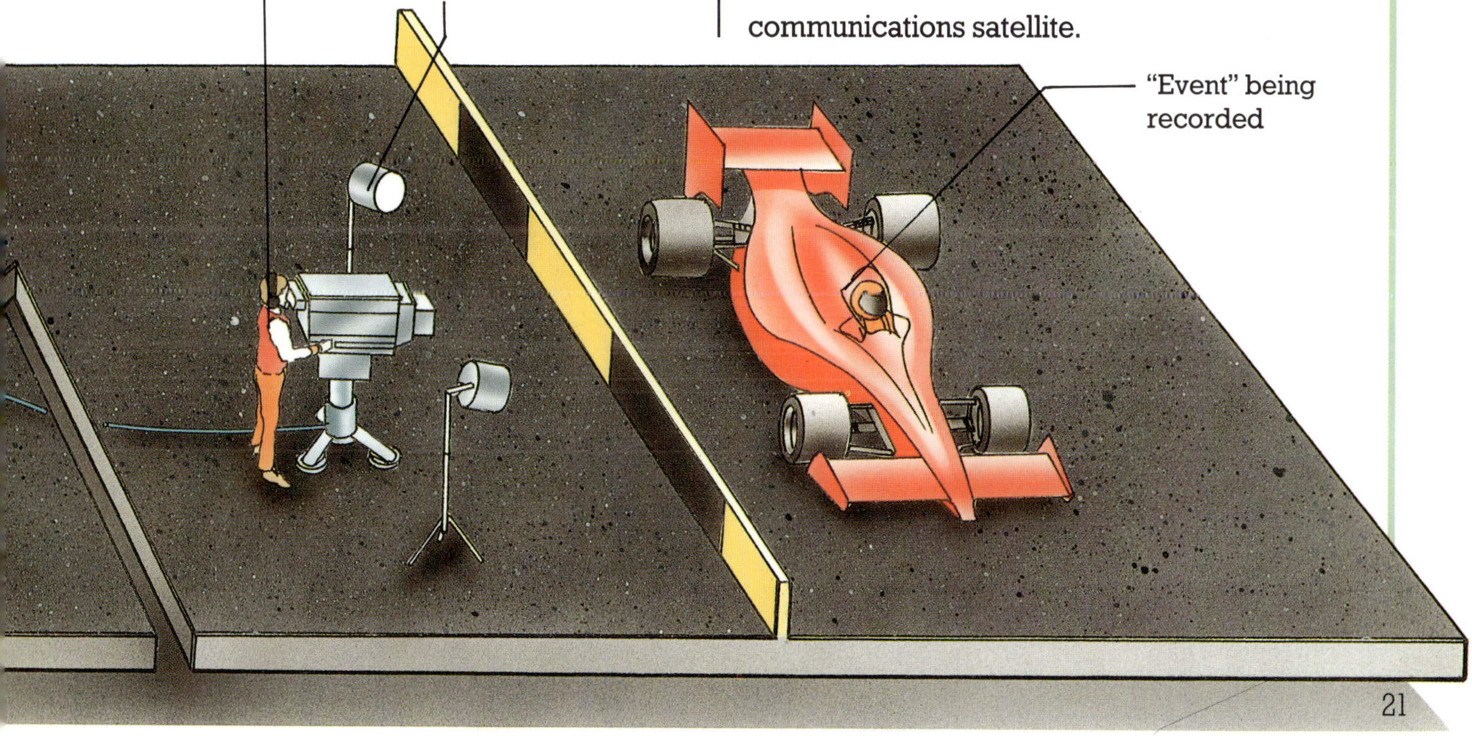

Cameraman

Lights

"Event" being recorded

SPECIAL EFFECTS

By processing a video or television signal electronically, the picture that appears on the screen can be altered to produce a range of special effects. Simple effects include changing the overall colour of the picture or turning it from a positive to a negative image, but considerably more ambitious and sophisticated effects are possible.

Multiple images and moving images may be created. The picture might be stretched, squeezed, spun round or flipped over. It can be distorted so that it changes from the flat screen shape into a rolling cylinder. Several images can be brought together to form a tumbling cube with a different image on each face. A picture may be exploded into a million tiny specks which blow around the screen like dust in the wind and then re-form as a totally different image.

The availability of inexpensive yet powerful computers has given rise to a new branch of special effects based on computer generated images and computer enhanced video images. Many TV adverts are now made using these.

The shape, colour and size of a television picture can be changed quite easily. The picture can be split up into any number of segments and each segment altered using a computer graphics system (below). Within such a set-up, the segments can be juggled around, some of them can be repeated at the expense of others, and segments from different programmes can be mixed together. Computer graphics can also form part of an ordinary TV broadcast (right) or the basis for a TV advert (below right).

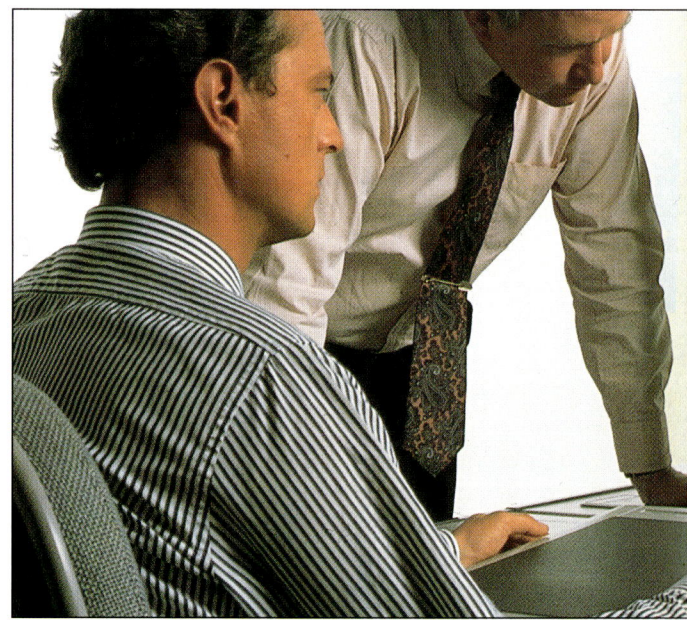

One very useful special effect is called chroma-key. An object, in this case a hot-air balloon, is viewed against a blue background by camera 1 (see A). Camera 2 shows an outdoor scene (B). The two images are mixed together (C) and the blue backing is removed so that the balloon appears to be flying through the mountainous scenery. Here, the three images for just one frame are shown, but the technique can be used for a sequence.

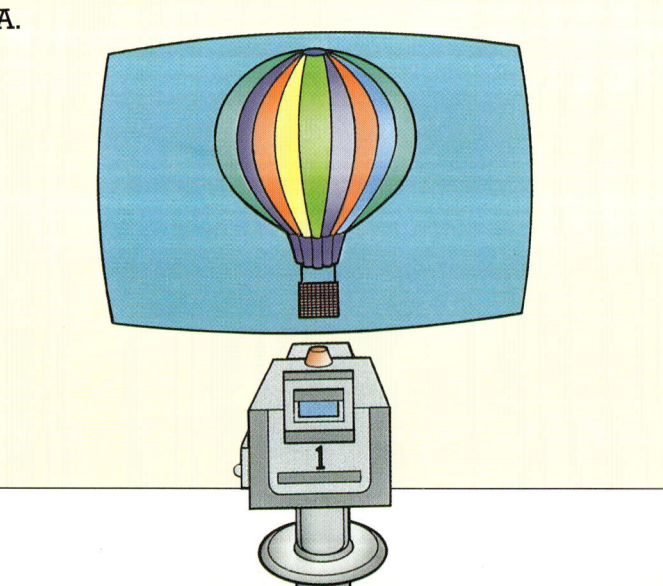

A.

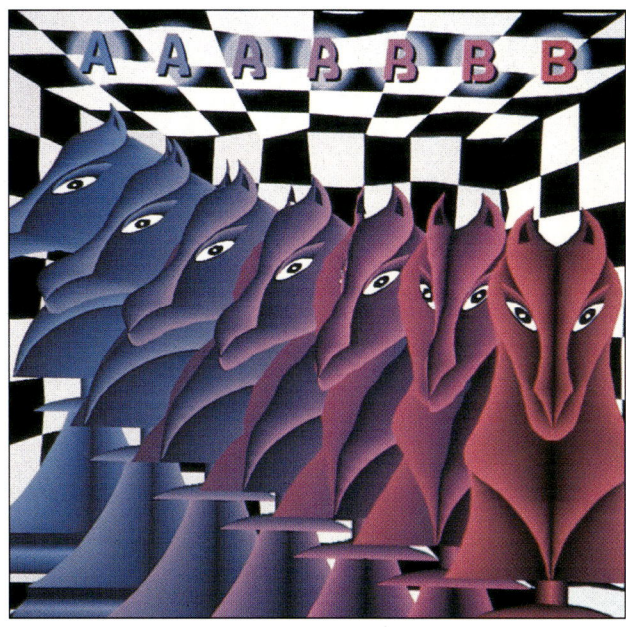
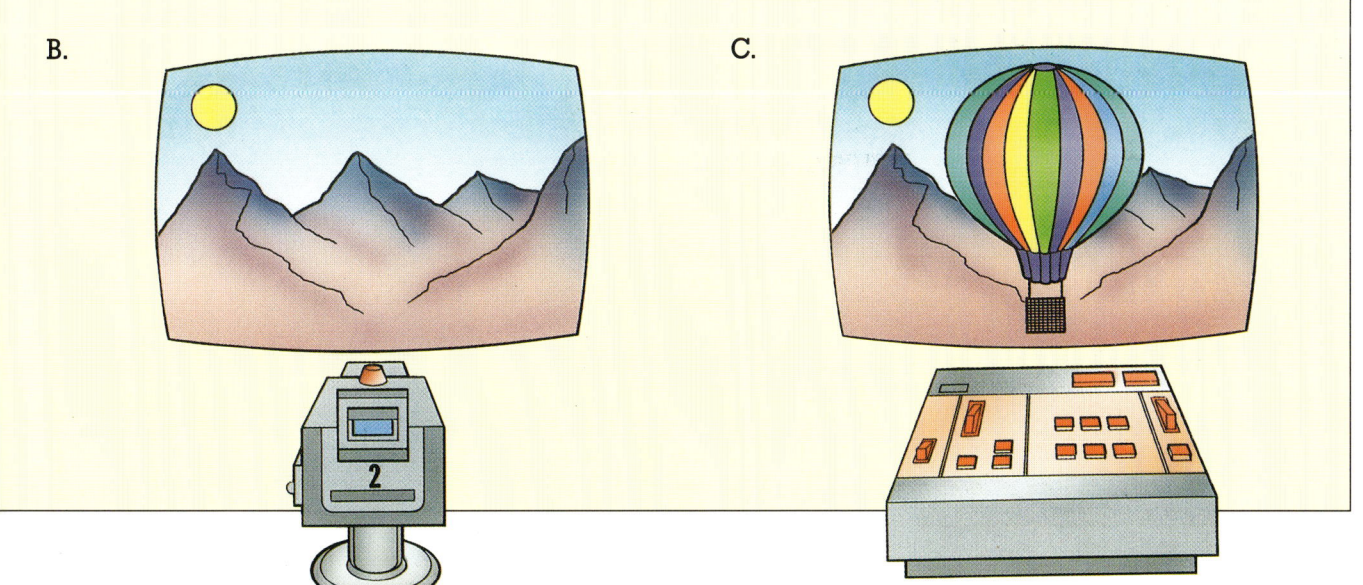

B.

C.

VIDEO DISCS

Television pictures can be recorded on discs as well as on tape. The laser disc stores information as microscopic pits burned into the disc. The pits form a track spiralling out from the centre of the disc. The disc is played by bouncing a narrow laser beam off it as it spins at up to 1,500 revolutions per minute. The beam is reflected strongly by the disc's silvery surface, but not by the pits. The flashing reflections are converted into an electrical signal which is then decoded into pictures and sound.

The laser beam does not have to follow the track all the way from beginning to end. It can be made to jump to any point on the disc within a second or so. This makes laser discs ideal for educational uses. Each student can choose a quite different combination of lessons and tests by responding to questions shown on the screen.

The BBC's Domesday Project in 1986 demonstrated the enormous amounts of information that laser discs can store and present in useful ways. The equivalent of over 300 books of maps, still and moving pictures, statistics, text and sounds about Britain are stored on just two 30cm laser discs. The Domesday discs are read by a laser disc player controlled by a computer.

The Domesday Project took two years to complete. One million people supplied data to it

To record on to a laser disc, television pictures and sound information are converted into electrical signals which control a laser. The laser beam burns pits in the disc in a pattern that matches the changing strength of the signals. To play the disc, it is scanned from underneath by a laser beam. The pits are tiny and there are billions of them on each disc. Tracking such pits on a disc spinning 1,500 times per second requires great precision.

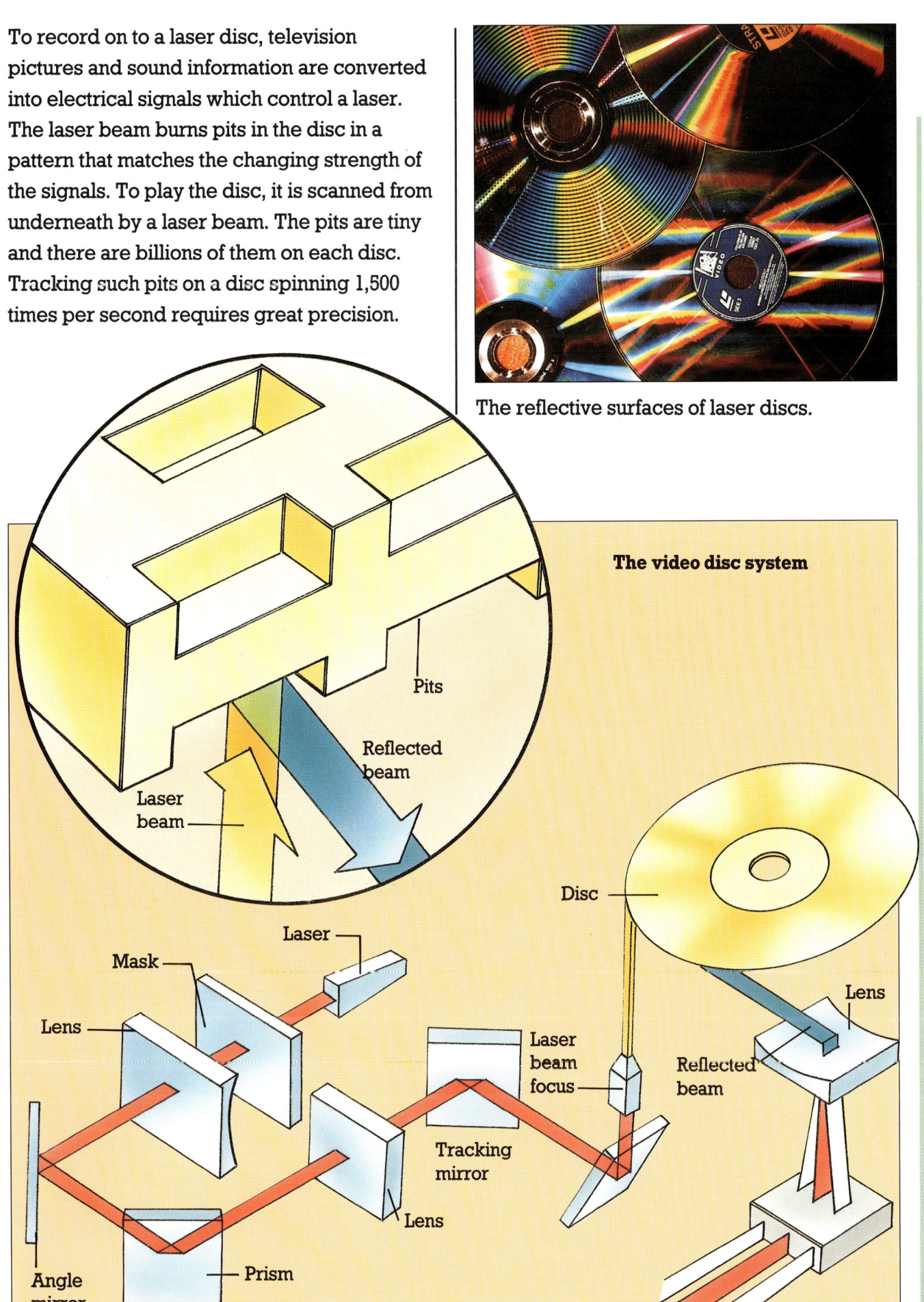

The reflective surfaces of laser discs.

The video disc system

SPECIAL SYSTEMS

Video and television technology is often combined with other types of equipment to produce specialized systems. Linking a video camera to a communications system enables video images to be sent from wherever the camera is to a more convenient place for viewing them. It enables dangerous places such as nuclear reactors to be monitored at a distance. Images are sent by cable from the camera to a viewing room where they can be looked at in safety. Linking video cameras to an industrial robot results in a robot that can see. By combining video and telephone technology, it is possible to make phones that enable callers to see each other.

The latest area of development, known as multimedia, involves the combination of video and home or office computer systems. With the right equipment and computer programs, video recordings can be mixed with computer text and graphics on a computer screen. Some multimedia systems enable live television pictures to be shown in a small panel, called a window, on a computer screen while the rest of the screen continues to run a computer program. Other systems enable live action and video stills from a laser disc to be incorporated in a computer game.

A mobile giant TV set shows adverts while on the move.

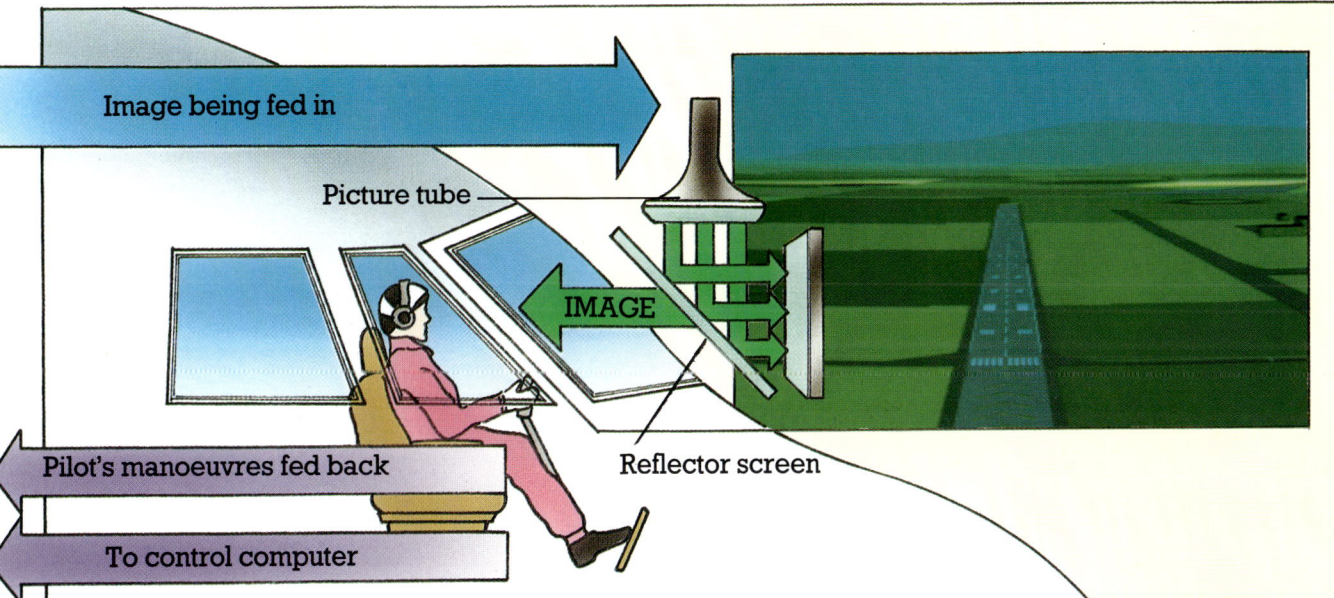

Flight simulators enable pilots to practice manoeuvres safely and without taking aircraft out of service. The pilot sits in a mock-up of the flight deck surrounded by moving computer generated images of the land and sky. Hydraulic rams move the flight deck according to the pilot's actions and sound effects make it sound realistic too. The pictures can be changed to copy the layouts and flight paths of many different airports.

A closed circuit TV (above) allows a security guard to monitor a doorway. Pictures of goods in a store, or text describing them, can be sent from a videotape or laser disc by telephone to a home computer (above right). The goods can be ordered and paid for by keying in a credit card number. A video camera mounted on a military robot (right) is used to look for bombs. A digitizer (left) converts images into digital code – a series of on/off or strong/weak signals – for processing by computer.

HISTORY OF TV AND VIDEO

The invention of the telephone in 1876 inspired scientists and inventors to look for ways of sending pictures by electricity. There were many suggestions as to how to do it, but the technology of the day was not able to turn them into working systems.

In 1907 in the Soviet Union, Boris Rosing used a cathode ray tube (CRT) to display crude outlines of shapes. A mechanical device changed the image into an electrical signal. This controlled a beam of electrons that made the CRT screen glow dimly. A British engineer, Alan Campbell Swinton, suggested using a beam of electrons to turn pictures into an electrical signal as well as to change it back into pictures in the CRT.

The first TV set designed by John Logie Baird.

The first successful television system was made by the Scottish inventor John Logie Baird. He transmitted the image of a Maltese cross to a tiny screen in February 1924 in Hastings, England. The world's first regular television broadcasts were made experimentally from Alexandra Palace, London, by the BBC in 1929 using Baird's system.

A Betamax video recorder, now obsolete.

The experimental service ended in 1935. In 1936 the Baird scan system, with its picture boosted from 30 lines to 240 lines per frame, was operated on alternate weeks with an all-electronic television system developed by the British EMI and Marconi companies. The EMI-Marconi system offered a better quality 405-line picture and more reliable cameras. Within three months the Baird system was discontinued.

All the early TV broadcasts had to be live because there was no way of recording them. In 1956 the US Ampex Corporation first recorded pictures and sound on 50mm-wide magnetic tape.

A 1980s TV set with remote control unit.

When the first communications satellites were launched in the 1960s, transatlantic broadcasts became possible. As the satellites became more powerful and could relay more television channels, transatlantic broadcasts became quite commonplace.

Satellites in orbit now transmit such powerful signals that these can be received by dish aerials only 45cm across. With a suitable aerial and receiver, every home can now watch programmes beamed down from space.

A modern compact lightweight camcorder.

Home video recorders first became available in the early 1970s. Different manufacturers created several different systems or formats. The Video Home System (VHS) developed by JVC became the most popular. Portable video equipment enabled people to make their own movies, but the equipment was heavy. The camera and recorder were separate units. By miniaturizing the equipment, camera and recorder were combined in a single lightweight unit, a camcorder.

Facts and figures

The first television sets, called Baird Televisors, went on sale in Britain in 1930 at a cost of 26 guineas, equivalent to £27.30 in decimal currency.

When the world's first regular 405-line television transmissions began from Alexandra Palace in London in 1936, there were an estimated 100 television sets in the United Kingdom.

The first domestic video recorder, the Philips N1500, went on sale in 1972.

The first transatlantic television broadcast by satellite took place on 11th July 1962. The transmission was relayed via the communications satellite Telstar and the picture showed the chairman of the company that owned the satellite.

The TV set that holds the record for the largest in the world is the Sony Jumbo Tron, which was shown at the Tsukuba International Exposition in Japan in 1985. The giant set measured 24.3m x 45.7m (80ft x 150ft).

At the other end of the scale, the smallest television set has a 30mm (1.2-inch) screen. The set, made by Seiko of Japan and introduced in 1982, came in three parts – a receiver, a screen on a wristband and headphones. The smallest one-piece set is the 6.85cm (2.7-inch) Casio-Keisanki TV-10 launched in 1983.

GLOSSARY

Betamax
A home video format developed in the mid-1970s by the Sony Corporation. Like its major rival at that time, VHS, Betamax used cassettes of 12.65mm (half-inch) wide tape. Betamax has been overtaken by the more popular VHS system developed by JVC.

DBS
Direct Broadcast by Satellite. Broadcasting television programmes from satellites travelling round, or orbiting, the Earth in a geostationary orbit. This is an orbit 36,000km from Earth in which a satellite's speed matches the Earth's and it appears to hover over the same place.

Fibre optics
Long, fine strands of glass used to transmit information in the form of an intense beam of light produced by a laser. The strands are bundled together to form fibre optic cables. Most cable television stations now use fibre optic cables instead of metal cables to feed television channels into people's homes.

Field
A television picture composed of half the normal number of scanning lines. Two fields form one complete picture.

Frame
A single complete television picture. 25 PAL frames and 30 NTSC frames are transmitted every second, a speed so fast that our eyes see them as a moving picture.

MAC
Multiplexed Analogue Components. The name of a new system for transmitting colour television signals. It offers better picture and sound quality than any of the older systems such as PAL and NTSC. MAC is used to broadcast some satellite television channels.

Microphone
A device for converting sounds into electrical signals.

NICAM
Near Instantaneous Companded Audio Multiplex. Nicam is a system developed in Britain by the BBC for transmitting television programmes with high-quality digital stereo sound.

NTSC
National Television Standards Committee. The committee that recommended the colour TV broadcasting system used throughout North America, most of South America, Japan and some Asian countries. The broadcasting system itself is also known as NTSC. NTSC pictures are each composed of 525 electron beam scanning lines and they are broadcast at the rate of 30 frames per second.

PAL
Phase Alternation by Line. The colour television broadcasting system used throughout most of Europe. PAL pictures are composed of 625 scanning lines and they are each broadcast at the rate of 25 frames per second.

SECAM
SEquentiel Couleur à Memoire. The colour TV broadcasting system used by France, the Soviet Union and some African and Middle East countries. SECAM pictures are each composed of 625 lines, broadcast at 25 per second.

Super VHS
A home video format developed from VHS offering improved picture quality

VCR
Video Cassette Recorder.

VHS
Video Home System, the world's most popular home video format developed by JVC in the mid-1970s. VHS uses cassettes of 12.65mm (half-inch) tape.

VHS-C
A development of VHS for portable equipment. A VHS-C tape cassette is smaller than a VHS cassette, enabling VHS-C camcorders to be made smaller and lighter than VHS ones. A VHS-C cassette can be played back in a VHS recorder just by slotting the smaller cassette into a VHS-size adaptor.

Video 8
A home video format developed by Sony in 1983. Video 8 uses cassettes of 8mm-wide tape. The smallness of the tape cassettes makes Video 8 particularly suitable for portable equipment. Video 8 camcorders are among the smallest and lightest.

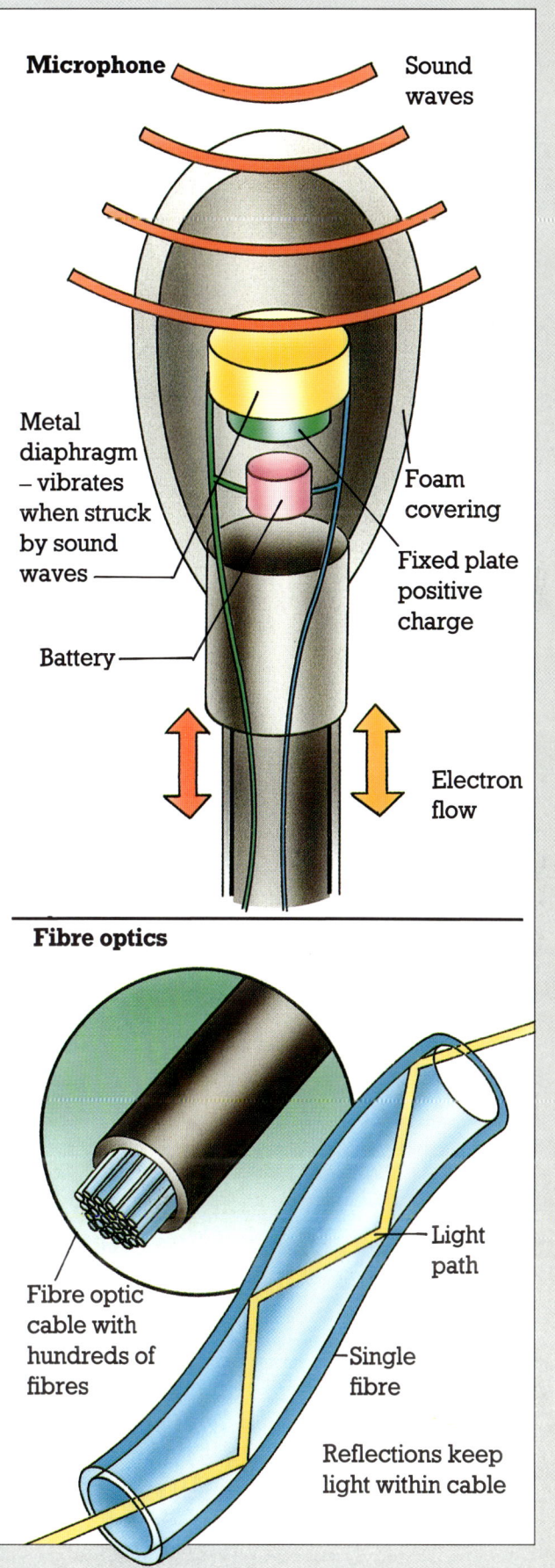

INDEX

aerials 12, 16, 17, 29

Baird, John Logie 28
batteries 7
BBC 24, 28
Betamax 28, 30
broadcasting and broadcasts 6, 12, 16, 18, 20, 28, 29, 30

cable television 16, 17, 21, 26
camcorder 5, 7, 12, 29
camera focusing system 5, 10
camera lens 5
cameras, TV 10, 11, 18, 19, 20
cameras, video 5, 7
carrier waves 12, 16
cathode ray tube 28
channels, TV 16
charge couple device (CCD) 5
chroma-key 22-23
colours, picture 8, 10, 11, 22, 23
computers and videos 12, 22, 24, 26, 27

digitizer 27
dish aerials 16, 17, 29
Domesday Project 24

editing tapes 15, 20
educational uses 7, 24
electrical signal conversions 5, 8, 11, 12, 16, 24, 25, 28
electromagnetic waves 16
electromagnets 10, 14
electronic news-gathering (ENG) 21
electrons and electron beams 8, 9, 10, 11, 16, 28

faceplate 11
fibre optic cables 16, 30, 31
field, picture 15, 29
flight simulator 27

games playing machines 12

home computer 12
home video 6, 7, 26, 29

images, changes to 22-23

laser discs 24-25, 26
light-sensitive materials 11
lines, screen 9, 28, 29

magnetic tape 4, 5, 14, 15
microphone 4, 30, 31
microwaves 20, 21
multimedia 26

news items 18, 20, 21
NICAM 30
NTSC 30

outside broadcasts 20, 21

PAL 30
phosphors 8, 9
pick-up tubes 5, 10, 11
picture and sound quality 6
portable equipment 6
power units 7
presenters, television 18
programmes 6, 12, 15, 16, 18, 19, 20

radio signals 12, 16, 20
recording pictures and sounds 5, 7, 14, 15, 24-25

relay satellites and stations 12, 16, 20
robots 26, 27

satellites, TV 12, 16, 17, 20, 28, 29
scanning 8, 9, 15
SECAM 31
shadow mask 8, 9
special effects 22-23

tape, recording 4, 12
target, camera 11
teleprompt 18
television camera 10, 11
television monitor/screen 5, 7, 8, 26
television set 5, 8, 9, 12, 28, 29
television picture signals 11, 12
television studio 18-19, 20
television viewing 6, 7
Telstar 29
timer, built-in recorder 6
transmitters 12, 16, 17, 21

VHS 15, 29, 30
video camera 5, 26
video discs 24-25
video heads 15
videophones 26
videotape 4, 14, 15
videotape cassettes 7
videotape recorder 5, 6, 12, 14, 29
viewfinder 4, 5
vision control room 19
vision mixer 19

Photographic credits
Cover and pages 7 top left and 12 top: Science Photo Library; page 6 top left: JVC Ltd; page 6 top right: Sanyo; pages 6 bottom, 9 both and 28 top: Roger Viltos; pages 7 top right, 15, 18 top and middle, 21 and 23 top: ITN Ltd; page 7 bottom: GEC Sensors; pages 10, 26 and 29: Sony UK; pages 12 bottom, 13 top, 23 bottom, 25 and 28 bottom: Lionheart Books; page 13 bottom: Philips; page 18 bottom: Autocue Ltd; pages 22-23: Quantel Engineering Facility; page 24: by permission of the BBC; page 27 top right: Prestel/British Telecom; page 28 middle: Popperfoto.